Dinosaurs

Story by Jenna Winterberg • Illustrations by Diana Fisher

Walter Foster®

Meet Nate. Nate is a Compsognathus, which is a type of dinosaur. Nate isn't just any old dinosaur— the Compsognathus is the smallest dinosaur to have ever roamed the Earth. This little guy is only about the size of a chicken, but that doesn't stop him from having big dreams!

Draw Nate the Compsognathus!

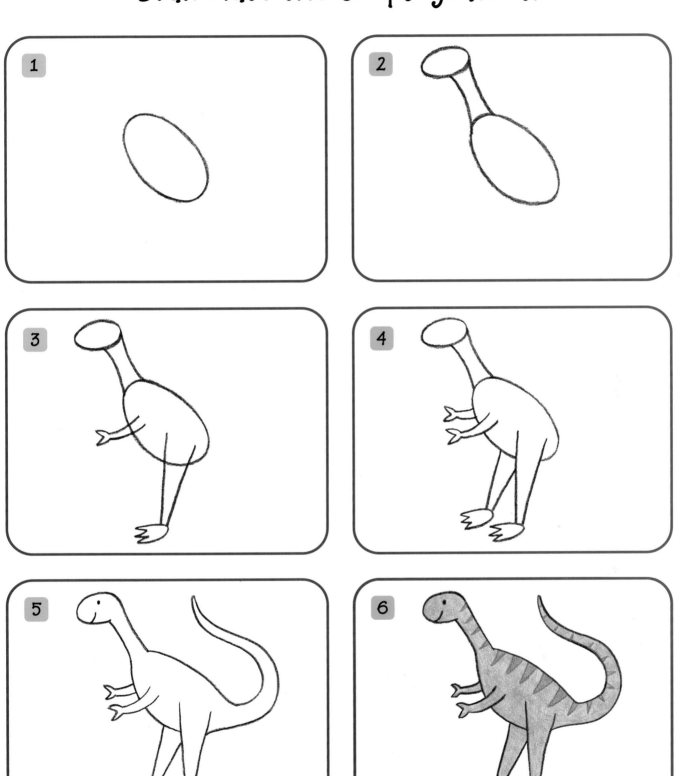

When you finish your drawing, place the sun sticker on the opposite page!

Nate's biggest dream is about to come true—he's going to compete in the Dinosaur Olympics! Many people believe that the ancient Greeks started the Olympic tradition, but the Greeks actually copied the dinosaurs. At least that's what the Apatosaurus who referees the track-and-field events tells Nate.

Draw the Apatosaurus!

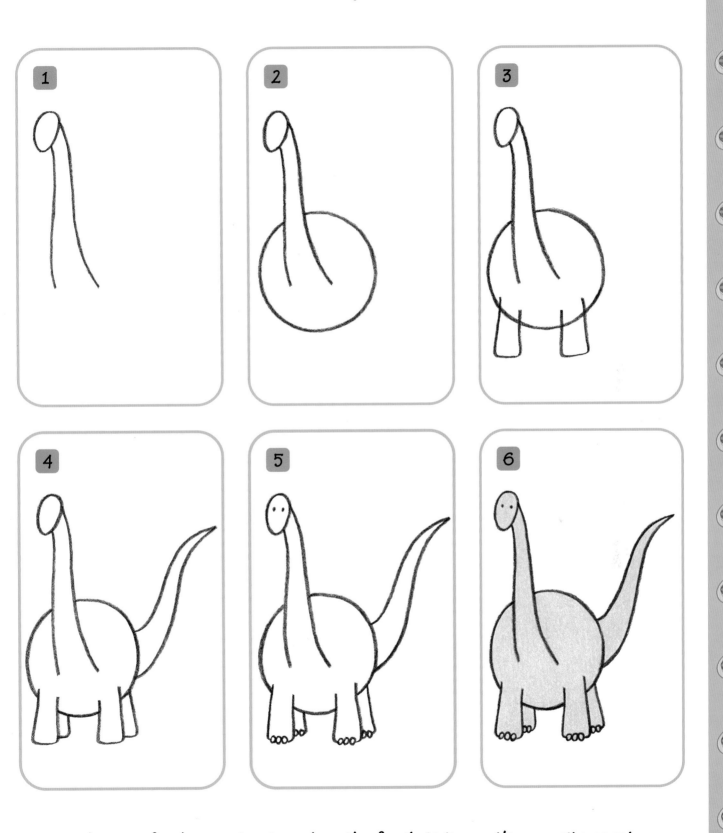

When you finish your drawing, place the fossil sticker on the opposite page!

Nate is very nervous about his first Olympics. And being the smallest dinosaur certainly doesn't help things, especially when it comes to events where size could make all the difference. But when Nate competes in the high jump, it isn't size that matters—it's wings! The Pterodactyl wins the gold.

Draw the Pterodactyl!

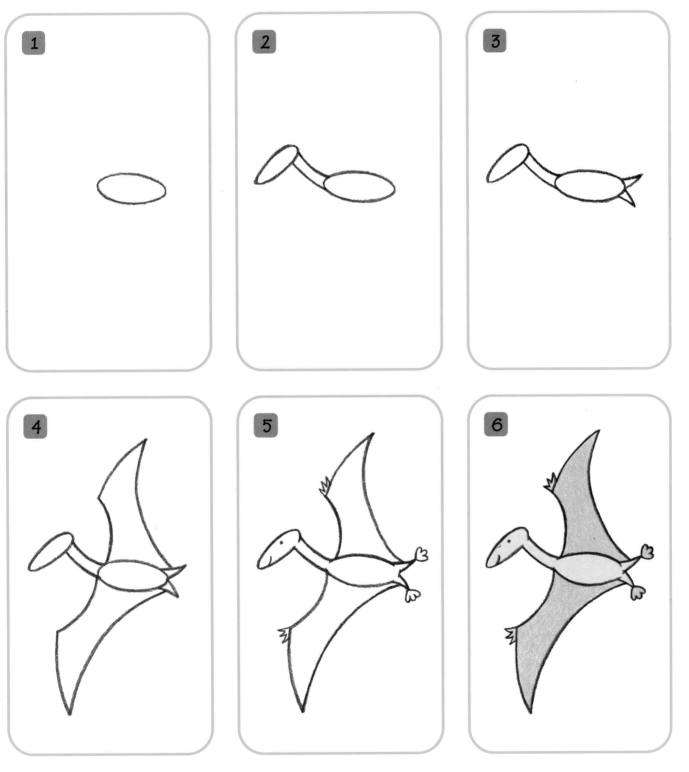

The long jump is next. Nate sizes up his competition. He looks up, up, up, and up some more. Next to him stands the tallest dinosaur ever—the 60-foot Sauroposeidon! This giant dino is so heavy that his jump causes an earthquake! It also wins him the gold.

Draw the Sauroposeidon!

When you finish your drawing, place the footprint sticker on the opposite page!

Nate is happy to be competing in the Olympics—but he really wants a gold medal! Nate thinks his small size might help him in the next event—the triple jump. But when the Triceratops swings her horned head as she jumps, all the other dinosaurs jump out of the way. The Triceratops wins the gold.

Draw the Triceratops!

When you finish your drawing, place the dragonfly sticker on the opposite page!

The next event—the shot put—requires a great deal of strength. Although Nate tries and tries, he can't even lift the giant rock, which is almost as big as he is! But the tough Ankylosaurus has no trouble wrapping his tail around the rock and sending it soaring through the sky. The Ankylosaurus earns the gold.

Reward Stickers

After finishing each drawing, encourage your child to complete the scene by choosing the appropriate sticker from the selection below!

Draw the Ankylosaurus!

When you finish your drawing, place the lizard sticker on the opposite page!

Next up is the event Nate knows he can win—the 100-meter dash, a short race emphasizing speed. Eagerly, Nate readies on his mark. But the race has barely begun when the Mamenchisaurus is declared the winner! As the dinosaur with the longest neck, Mamenchisaurus finds it an easy stretch to the gold.

Draw the Mamenchisaurus!

1

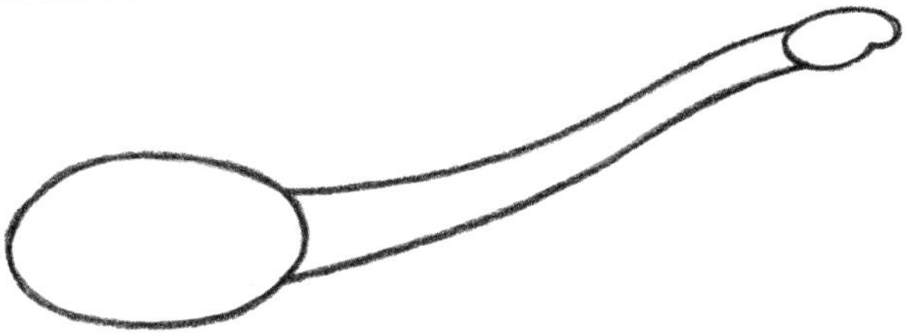

2

3

4

5

When you finish your drawing, place the dinosaur nest sticker on the opposite page!

Nate is determined to win an event in the Dinosaur Olympics—and the long-distance race could be the one! Because the large dinosaurs get tired easily, this race favors the small ones. Sure enough, a little dino wins—but it's the quick-footed Ornithomimus, not Nate, who takes home the gold.

Draw the Ornithomimus!

When you finish your drawing, place the snake sticker on the opposite page!

Nate is discouraged, but he hasn't given up hope. The steeplechase is an obstacle course event that requires speed and agility—skills Nate has because of his small size. But Nate doesn't have the strength and endurance of the brawny Stegosaurus, who is protected from the rough course by a tough body of armor. She wins the gold medal.

Draw the Stegosaurus!

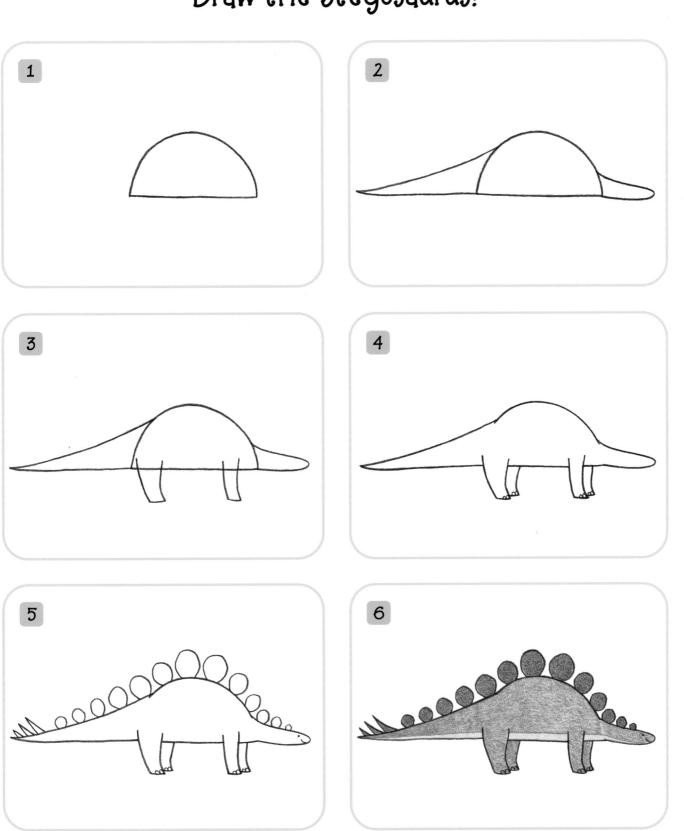

When you finish your drawing, place the comet sticker on the opposite page!

The relay race is next. Nate teams up with some Compsognathus cousins. If they work together, they're sure they can win the competition! Encouraged, Nate runs as fast as he can. Meanwhile, the Diplodocus dinosaurs stand still and pass the baton with their long, limber tails. The Diplodocus win the gold.

Draw the Diplodocus!

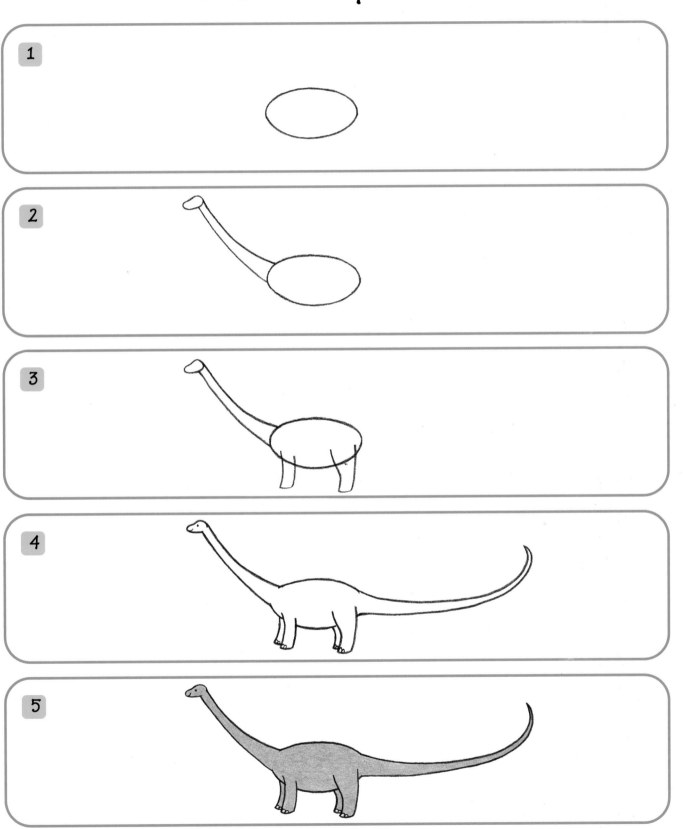

1

2

3

4

5

When you finish your drawing, place the Pterodactyl sticker on the opposite page!

With his head hung low, Nate approaches the last event— the hurdles. Nate is so focused on losing, he doesn't immediately recognize that he's standing next to a Tyrannosaurus rex. Terrified, Nate takes off in a blur and wins the race! The audience roars in appreciation when the littlest dinosaur is awarded the gold!

Draw the Tyrannosaurus rex!

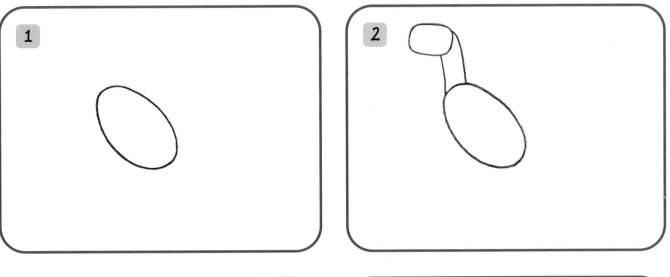

1

2

3

4

5

6

When you finish your drawing, place the hidden dinos sticker on the opposite page!

The end.